Book 7

Ick and Crud

The Big Snow

by Wiley Blevins • illustrated by Jim Paillot

RED CHAIR
·PRESS·

Funny Bone Books

and Funny Bone Readers are produced and published by
Red Chair Press LLC   PO Box 333   South Egremont, MA 01258-0333
www.redchairpress.com

About the Author

Wiley Blevins has taught elementary school in both the United States and South America. He has also written over 60 books for children and 15 for teachers, as well as created reading programs for schools in the U.S. and Asia with Scholastic, Macmillan/McGraw-Hill, Houghton-Mifflin Harcourt, and other publishers. Wiley currently lives and writes in New York City.

About the Artist

Jim Paillot is a dad, husband and illustrator. He lives in Arizona with his family and two dogs and any other animal that wants to come in out of the hot sun. When not illustrating, Jim likes to hike, watch cartoons and collect robots.

Publisher's Cataloging-In-Publication Data

Names: Blevins, Wiley. | Paillot, Jim, illustrator.
Title: Ick and Crud. Book 7, The big snow / by Wiley Blevins; illustrated by Jim Paillot.
Other Titles: Big snow | Funny bone books. First chapters.

Description: South Egremont, MA : Red Chair Press, [2019] | Series: Funny bone books. First chapters | Summary: "Ick and Crud are surprised when duty calls them outside and they discover the first big snowfall of the season. The two pals enjoy the snow, but then Bob, the human takes them to the neighbor's house to warm up. Readers will enjoy the surprises as the canine crew can't wait to get home."

Identifiers: ISBN 9781634402637 (library hardcover) | ISBN 9781634402675 (paperback) | ISBN 9781634402712 (ebook)

Subjects: LCSH: Friendship--Juvenile fiction. | Snow--Juvenile fiction. | Dogs--Juvenile fiction. | CYAC: Friendship--Fiction. | Snow--Fiction. | Dogs--Fiction.

Classification: LCC PZ7.B618652 Icb 2019 | DDC [E]--dc23 | LCCN 2017963420

Printed in the United States of America
1018 1P CGBS19

Table of Contents

 1 Snow Angels............. 5

 2 Playing Fun-with-Bob...... 12

3 Hot Chocolate
and Treats 19

4 The Cat That Stares 24

Meet the Characters

Crud

Ick

Miss Puffy

Bob

Snow Angels

"**H**urry," said Bob. He opened the door.
"It's time for you-know-what."

Ick and Crud raced outside. Ick ran
to the right. Crud waddled to the left.
Each searched for that just-right spot.
But where was it?

The ground sat covered in a blanket of white. Little flakes fell from the sky.

"Catch them with your tongue," said Crud.

"Catch what?" asked Ick.

"The snowflakes."

"The cupcakes?" asked Ick. "Yum!"

"No," said Crud. "Look up."

Ick tilted his head and stuck
out his tongue. "I missed," he cried.

"Try again," said Crud.

Ick stuck out his tongue once more.
A big snowflake plopped on it. "Nice!"
he said. "It's fluffy and crunchy at the
same time. I wish I was a snowflake."

"Me, too," said Crud. "Here comes
another big one."

Ick raced to catch it.

His left feet went right. His right feet
went left. He flipped and flapped his legs
as fast as he could.

"Look," said Crud, as Ick lifted himself.
"You made a snow angel."

"*Ooh!*" said Ick. "Let's make some more."

The two flipped and flopped on the snow. Each flapped his legs. Then they got up and flipped and flopped somewhere else. Before long the yard was filled with doggie snow angels.

"We made art," said Ick.

"We made something," said Crud.

"Something beautiful," whispered Ick.

"Hey, Ick," said Crud. "Don't look now, but someone is watching us."

"Where?" said Ick as he spun to look around.

"Smooth move," said Crud.

Miss Puffy sat in the window. She licked her paws like they were icy lollipops. She leaned in and hissed at them. Her breath made a big foggy spot on the window. Before it could disappear, she lifted her paw and made a big X on it.

"What does that mean?" asked Ick.

Crud rolled his eyes. "I think it's her name."

"Oh," said Ick. "I'm cold."

"Yeah," said Crud. "Let's go in, buddy."

Ick scratched at the front door.

"We're freezing our doggie paws out here!" barked Crud.

"Yeah," moaned Ick.

"Wait," said Crud. "We forgot to do you-know-what."

"Oh, right," said Ick.

Just then Bob opened the door. He grabbed their collars. And it was too late.

Playing Fun-with-Bob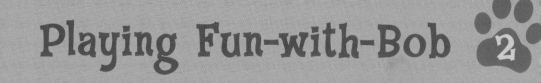

Bob squatted in front of the TV. Ick and Crud found spots next to him. "A big storm is coming," he said. "Looks like we might be stuck at home for a while."

Crud look at Ick. "You know what that means, don't you?"

"Yes," said Ick. Then he lifted his head. "What does that mean?"

"It means Fun-with-Bob time," said Crud.

"Oh, I love Fun-with-Bob time," said Ick.
"How do we play Fun-with-Bob again?"

"First, we play Scare-Bob."

"Oh, that *is* fun," said Ick. "Then what?"

"Then we play Hide-from-Bob."

"Yes," said Ick. "That's my favorite."

"Are you ready, buddy?" asked Crud.

"I will if you will," said Ick.

Both jumped up and stared into the air. Crud twisted his head side to side. Ick twisted and twitched from front to back. Bob shot up.

"What's wrong, boys?"

Crud ran and stared under the couch. He let out a deep growl. Ick ran in circles, yelp-yelp-yelping.

Bob scrunched down. He inched
toward the couch. Then slowly he peeked
underneath it.

"There's nothing here, boys," said Bob.
He lifted his head. But Ick and Crud were
nowhere to be seen.

"Where are you boys?" asked Bob.

Bob went from room to room. No Crud. No Ick. Then he spotted a little tail poking from under a curtain. It wiggled back and forth.

Bob tip-toed to the curtain. "1, 2, 3... A-ha!" he yelled, pushing back the curtain. But nothing was there.

Ick and Crud had slipped underneath the puffy blanket on the couch. "Don't move, buddy," whispered Crud. Ick shook his head.

"Crud! Ick!" yelled Bob. "Where are you?" They could hear his footsteps coming closer. *Clop. Clop. Clop.*

Just then a feather from the blanket drifted on Ick's nose. "Don't do it, buddy," whispered Crud. Ick poked his head from under the blanket and shook off the feather. Then he slid under the blanket again. But it was too late. *Ah-ah-choooo!* Off flew the blanket.

Bob stood over them shaking his head. "Nice try, boys," he said. "Maybe you two need to go outside again."

"Yes!" barked Ick and Crud.

Hot Chocolate and Treats

Outside, the snow had quickly piled up. Ick hopped into a big fluffy pile.

"Where are you, buddy?" asked Crud.

"Here," yelled Ick. He poked out his head. "Why is it so cold?"

"It's snow," said Crud. "Frozen water."

"Oh," said Ick. "Maybe we can find warmer snow somewhere else."

They headed out of the yard and down
the sidewalk with Bob. Just then a big
blue hat popped over the fence.

"Hello, Bob," said Mrs. Martin.
"Nice day for a walk." Bob laughed.

"I made some fresh hot chocolate.
Come on in. I'm sure Ick and Crud would
like to warm up."

Miss Puffy stood in the doorway.
She arched her back and hissed. Each
hiss turned into little bits of ice and fell
at her feet.

"Oh, no, no, no," said Crud.

"Not gonna go in there," said Ick.
"No way. No how!" They turned and
headed back down the sidewalk.

"Come on, boys. Don't make me carry you in." Bob tugged on Crud's collar. He grabbed at Ick's. But Ick was faster. He jumped into another pile of fluffy snow. And disappeared beneath it.

"Gotcha!" yelled Bob. He pulled out Ick and tucked him under his arm.

Mrs. Martin stood in the doorway. "I have fresh-baked treats, too," she said. "Ick and Crud can have as many as they want!"

Ick leaped out of Bob's arms. Crud jumped up and did a flip. Then the two raced into Mrs. Martin's house, past a hissing Miss Puffy, and straight to the place that smelled so good. The kitchen.

"What is this?" asked Ick.

"I've never... oh-whoa-wow... never, never, never seen anything like it," said Crud.

Everywhere they looked was a cat. A cat cookie jar. Cat oven mitts. Cat cups and glasses. Cat towels. Even cat paw prints on the walls.

"This has to be the worst place on Earth," said Crud.

"Yes," said Ick. "The worst."

"Maybe it'll be better in another room," said Crud. Ick followed as he waddled into the next room.

But it was filled with cat pillows.
Cat curtains. Cat-shaped flower pots.
And cat pictures all over the wall.

"Oh, ick," said Ick.

"Oh, yes," said Crud. "This is even
worse!"

Miss Puffy perched on a small
table, flipping her tail from side to side.
Underneath was a golden cat statue.
Beside it was a smaller, furry cat.

"Is it real?" asked Ick.

"I don't know, buddy," said Crud. "Its eyes aren't moving."

"But they're staring right at us," moaned Ick.

Crud barked. The cat didn't move.

"It didn't even meow," said Ick. "But it looks so real."

"I know," said Crud. "You sneak beside it, tap it, and see what happens."

"Why me?" asked Ick.

"You're the smallest," said Crud.

"But what if it bites?" Or scratches? Or sneezes on me? I'm too young to get some weird cat disease. I'm too pretty to grow cat whiskers. I'm too..."

"Just go," said Crud. "I'll distract her."

Ick squatted low to the floor. He wiggled and squiggled toward the cat with the staring eyes. Meanwhile, Crud stood on two legs and barked. He turned and wiggled. "Stop making me laugh," whispered Ick.

Then Crud hopped on one leg and tried to dance a little jig. The cat just stared and stared.

"Almost there," whispered Ick. "Keep dancing, or whatever you call that."

"I... I... I can't," yelled Crud. Plop!

Crud rolled left. Then he rolled right. He rolled and rolled until he rolled into Ick. Ick flipped and landed on top of the staring cat. The cat flew from under him and hit the golden cat statue. It toppled over and CRASH! Tiny golden cat pieces scattered everywhere.

"Oh, crud," said Crud.

"Oh, no," said Ick.

The two raced to the front door.
Mrs. Martin stood there with the door
already open. Bob followed them out.
"Send me the bill," he shouted as he
waved goodbye. Miss Puffy let out a long
hiss that sounded more like a giggle. Ick
and Crud sped down the sidewalk, through
the piles of snow, and into their yard.

And just before Bob could open the door, they both found the perfect spot for you-know-what.

"I'm sure glad we're home," said Ick.

"Yes," said Crud. "There's no better place to be than a cat-free home on a snowy day!"